READ ALL OF
AXEL & BEAST'S
ADVENTURES!

AXEL & BEAST

ROBOTIC RUMBLE

ADRIAN C. BOTT ART BY ANDY ISAAC

Kane Miller
A DIVISION OF EDC PUBLISHING

First American Edition 2017
Kane Miller, A Division of EDC Publishing

Text Copyright © Adrian C Bott 2017
Illustration Copyright © Andy Isaac 2017
First published in Australia by Hardie Grant Egmont 2017

For information contact:
Kane Miller, A Division of EDC Publishing
P.O. Box 470663
Tulsa, OK 74147-0663
www.kanemiller.com
www.edcpub.com
www.usbornebooksandmore.com

Library of Congress Control Number: 2016955654

Printed and bound in the United States of America
1 2 3 4 5 6 7 8 9 10

ISBN: 978-1-61067-636-6

CHAPTER 1

The house where Axel and his mother, Nedra, lived was already fairly small, so when Aunt Vicki and the five cousins came for one of their summer visits, it was like living in a mouse's sock drawer.

Axel perched on the arm of the couch. He had to.

The rest of the couch was taken up with a fight between the **sticky-faced** twins,

Sara and Hunter, who were yelling and struggling over Axel's single game controller.

Out in the backyard, shaggy-haired Kyle was striding back and forth **shouting** into his phone: "Dave is **out** of the band. I mean it, Steve. He's **out** this time and that's final!"

Little Milo was temporarily imprisoned beneath a large upturned laundry basket for his own safety and Amali was dancing on the upstairs landing, singing her way through her musical theater collection. Axel didn't dislike *Wicked*, *Matilda* or *Aladdin*, but he had heard them all a few too many times this week.

Axel looked gloomily out of the front window at Aunt Vicki's camper parked in the driveway. That was where the cousins were *supposed* to sleep, but somehow they all migrated indoors before the visit was over, **every single time.** Having kids sleeping all over the place made it impossible for him to sneak through the house after dark.

I haven't been able to check on BEAST in days, he thought. *I hope he's okay.*

BEAST, Axel's best friend, was a shape-shifting robot who lived in a **secret den** beneath the backyard. Together Axel and BEAST went on missions against Grabbem

Industries, the **evil mega-corporation.** Grabbem wanted to secretly plunder Earth's resources and didn't care how much destruction they caused.

Kyle didn't know it, but he was **stomping** around above BEAST's head at this very moment. If Axel pressed the remote control switch in his pocket, the metal doors hidden beneath the lawn would open and cousin Kyle would suddenly find himself falling into the secret den.

There was another way into the den: a curtained-off hole in the cellar wall. Axel wasn't too worried about any of the cousins finding it. Nobody ever went down to the cellar, except to do the laundry or fetch something from the freezer.

"It's my turrrrn!" screamed Sara. Axel winced as the sticks on his beloved game controller were tugged and twisted.

"Why don't we all play something else?" he said. "Or we could all go for, um, a walk or something? Outside?"

"I WANT TO PLAY DIGGY BLOCKS!" bawled Hunter. "I HADN'T FINISHED BUILDING MY **TOILET CASTLE!**"

Axel buried his head in his hands. He didn't even want to know what a "toilet castle" was.

From upstairs came only silence for a moment. Then a voice sang out: "*Naaaaaaaants ingonYAma bagithi Babaaaa!*"

Amali had reached the *Lion King* soundtrack. Yesterday Axel had found her leaning over the balcony railing, solemnly lifting one of Axel's old teddies over her head.

Kyle yelled something into the phone and then shot a glance at Axel through the window. The message was clear: *You didn't hear that.*

Axel scowled at him. For a sweet second he imagined pressing the control switch, just to see the look on Kyle's face as he fell through the lawn.

"I want to play zombies!" Sara squealed. **"DIGGY BLOCKS!"** screeched Hunter. His screeches had gone beyond fingernails-on-a-chalkboard noises and now sounded like a pterodactyl playing the violin.

Axel wondered, in a vague kind of way, if his cousin's voices could get any **screechier.** And if so, which one's head would **explode** first?

Watching the twins was a headache, but it was better than being in the kitchen, where his mom and Aunt Vicki were talking about his dad. Axel didn't want to hear Aunt Vicki talk about "moving on" or "accepting reality." He knew, just like his mom knew, that Matt

Brayburn was still alive out there somewhere … and that one day, he would come home.

In his mind, Axel left the screaming and the chaos behind and followed his memory back to the day his father had gone missing.

Matt Brayburn had gone to pick up some takeout for dinner and had never come back. They had found his car upside down beside the road, without a scratch on it. It hadn't rolled or crashed. It was just upside down …

Amali came flying down the stairs, her long hair streaming behind her like a goth-black **Comet** trail. "Axel? Where's Milo?"

Axel looked at the toppled-over laundry basket. There was no sign of Milo.

"Oh no. He got out!"

The kitchen door flew open. "Milo's gone?" gasped Aunt Vicki. "Weren't you supposed to be watching him?"

Axel desperately looked around the room. Milo wasn't hiding behind the TV or mountaineering on the couch. Amali would have seen him if he'd gone upstairs. The glass sliding door to the garden was closed. That only left …

Axel's eyes widened in **horror** as he saw the cellar door standing ajar.

From the cellar came a piercing squeal – not of fright, but of joy …

"WOBOT!"

"Axel!" hissed Nedra.

"Wait, Milo! Mommy's coming!" shouted Aunt Vicki.

She lunged for the cellar door, but Axel got there first. He ran down the steps.

There, under a bare light bulb, with the pulled-back curtain in his hand and a huge grin on his face, was Milo.

"Mommy, look! I found a weally big WOBOT!" Milo shouted. **"He's 'normous!** I want to play wiv him!"

Axel could see all the way through to the secret den. BEAST was cowering right at the back, his eyes flickering apologetically.

"He's found one of Axel's old toys, I think," said Aunt Vicki from the top of the stairs. "Some sort of robot."

"Toy robot? I want it!" yelled Hunter.

"No, me!" yelled Sara.

"Iss NOT a toy," Milo shouted, and stamped his foot. "Iss a BIG wobot. I maked him happy. I want to plaaaay wiv him."

BEAST looked at Axel in a pleading way. Axel noticed that BEAST had a smile drawn on his face, in what looked like **red crayon.**

"What's going on down there?" asked Aunt Vicki suspiciously.

She started down the cellar steps.

With one swift motion, Axel grabbed Milo with one hand and tugged the curtain closed with the other. He lifted his little cousin up and gave him a hug. An idea had popped into his brain.

"Come on. Let's go and tell everyone about the big robot."

"Yay!" said Milo.

Aunt Vicki and the cousins all looked on with curious faces as Axel came back through the cellar door holding Milo in his arms.

"We've got something amazing to share with you. You all have to keep it **top secret.** There's a giant robot in the cellar," he told them in a whisper. "It's black and green, and its eyes light up."

"Yess!" said Milo happily.

Kyle rolled his eyes and went back outside.

Aunt Vicki gave Axel a slow, understanding smile. "Well! Aren't you lucky to have a giant robot! Does he have a **death ray?**"

"Oh, no," said Axel. "He doesn't want to hurt anyone. He's a nice robot, isn't he, Milo?"

"I fink he must be," Milo said thoughtfully.

Hunter and Sara looked disgusted. "It's just a game they're playing," Sara said. "There's no robot." She flung herself back on the couch.

Vicki took Milo back from Axel's arms and kissed his head. "He's really good with the little ones, isn't he, Neds?" she said to her sister. "He's got Milo entranced!"

"Yeah, Axel's always had a brilliant imagination," said Nedra. She and Axel shared a *that-was-too-close* look.

"He'll make a great dad one day, eh?" said Vicki. "Got a girlfriend yet, Ax?"

"I don't think Axel's dating decisions are any of our business," said Nedra, her jaw tight.

Axel's phone **pinged.**

"Excuse me," he said, relieved to get away from the conversation.

Out in the front garden he saw who had messaged him and his heart lurched. It was Agent Omega, his undercover friend at Grabbem Industries.

Axel. Need U + BST 2 get 2 Foxley Woods right away. Will explain l8r. Omega

P.S. Can U learn how to read Japanese in the next 10 mins?

CHAPTER 2

Foxley Woods was a spooky little scrap of woodland just outside of town. It was the kind of place where only teenagers and lost hikers ever went. Using GOPHER, BEAST's tunneling underground form, Axel reached it in minutes.

They burst up from the ground into a wide clearing. Overhead, the sky was growing dark, and the thick tree cover made the clearing even darker. There wasn't another human being in sight.

Axel's neck hair prickled with anticipation.

A ghostly green light appeared, shining between the trees. Something **big** was out there, and it was coming their way. Axel held his breath as he watched it come into view.

It was a craft of some kind, shaped like a white ball with round windows in its sides, and with dozens of drooping metal tentacles hanging down from underneath.

It hovered in eerie silence and then drifted toward them like a **jellyfish.** As it came closer, Axel realized it was big enough to swallow BEAST whole.

"What *is* that?" he whispered.

"I CANNOT MOVE," said BEAST. "UNKNOWN CRAFT IS TAKING OVER MY CIRCUITS!"

Axel grabbed the controls and tried to pull BEAST back, away from the oncoming apparition. But the robot wouldn't budge ... and now the hovering ball thing started rising above them, like a balloon. Axel saw there was a hole in the bottom of it, among the tentacles.

"Stay calm," said a voice over BEAST's communicator. "This is all part of the standard docking procedure."

"Agent Omega!" Axel said in relief. "Is that you in there?"

The ball craft descended slowly, then stopped, hovering above them. **Tentacles** latched on to BEAST's limbs. The next moment, all of his energy levels began to rise.

"OOH," BEAST said happily. "THAT TICKLES."

As they were drawn up into the ship, Axel saw Agent Omega standing by a guardrail, waving at him.

"Welcome on board," said Agent Omega. "Hope I didn't alarm you just now."

The opening beneath them hissed shut. BEAST's chest panel popped open by itself. Agent Omega reached out a hand to Axel and helped him onto the walkway. The craft was small, but its entire inner surface was covered with screens, readouts and technical gadgetry.

"This beauty is called the MOT-BOL," Omega said. "Not much of a name, I know.

It stands for **Mobile Observation, Tactics and Battle Optimization Laboratory.** I've borrowed it from Grabbem."

"Borrowed?" Axel laughed.

"On a permanent basis," said Omega with a grin. "The MOT-BOL is an experimental mobile repair and prep craft for **shifters** like BEAST here. We can use it to take him places, recharge his power cells, and even repair him if he gets damaged."

Axel couldn't remember the last time he'd seen Agent Omega this happy. "So you'll be coming with us on missions now? Won't Grabbem get suspicious if you're gone for too long?"

"I'm on extended leave," said Omega, grinning even wider. "According to Grabbem's computers, which I wouldn't dream of hacking,

I've come down with the Manticorian flu. Highly contagious."

He tapped on a keyboard built into the wall. A blue light lit up with a **ping** and a compartment opened with a puff of super-cold vapor. Inside were two cans of soda. He passed one to Axel and took the other himself.

"We can use the MOT-BOL to deploy BEAST anywhere in the world," he explained. "You won't need to use SHARKOS and SKYHAWK as much now, and you'll have a bolt-hole to retreat to when you're on missions."

"Meatball," said Axel thoughtfully.

"Say what?"

"It's round. It has all that metal spaghetti underneath. It's not a MOT-BOL, it's a **Meatball!**"

Agent Omega stroked his chin. "Meatball. I like it."

"So," said Axel, sipping his drink, "why did you ask me to learn to read Japanese? I didn't, by the way."

"Because we're going to Japan." Agent Omega's smile vanished. He slowly pushed a lever, and the Meatball hummed up into the sky. "To a place where no living person has set foot in years. They call it **Ghost Island.**"

Agent Omega folded a panel down from the wall and motioned for Axel to do the same. The panel turned into a padded seat. Axel **boggled** at how neatly everything fit away inside the Meatball. There was probably a dining table in here somewhere. Complete with an eighteen-piece dinner set.

"Get comfortable," Omega said. "I'm going to tell you a story."

"ARE THERE GHOSTS IN IT?" asked BEAST, with a tiny quiver in his voice.

"We'll come to that. Once upon a time, a brilliant scientist called Doctor Minamoto invented an experimental reactor, the Phoenix. It turned matter into energy. Though it was no bigger than this soda can, it was so crazy-effective it could turn one grain of rice into enough electricity to power a city for a week."

Axel said, "Whoa. I bet Grabbem would love to get their hands on that."

"Them and me both! However, the Phoenix had one big problem. It was unstable, and it was **hungry.** The more energy it produced, the more it wanted. If it was left running, it would soon start to suck in everything around it and turn *that* into energy, too. The result ... *boom.*"

"BIG BOOM," echoed Axel.

"Exactly. So the Phoenix Reactor was sealed in a vault and buried deep underground in a secret location."

Agent Omega drew Axel's attention to a screen across from them. It showed a lonely looking island in the middle of a gray sea.

"Zoom in," commanded Omega.

The view suddenly showed a deserted city, stretching out into the distance. Towering, empty buildings overlooked silent streets. There were cars in the streets, but none of them moved. The city seemed **frozen in time.**

"Ghost Island used to be a mining station. A city grew above the ground, where thousands of workers and their families lived. But then it was abandoned," said Agent Omega. "The official reason was some kind of radiation leak, but people soon started to tell other stories. Like the one about the ghostly monster."

"CAN AGENT OMEGA TELL US A

DIFFERENT STORY, PLEASE?" said BEAST. His ear antennae **drooped** and he looked scared.

"Sorry, BEAST. We need to hear this," said Axel.

Agent Omega went on: "Apparently the mines were dug too deep and they disturbed some kind of radioactive **dragon-ghost-monster thing,** and that's why everyone bailed. Now, I think that story's faker than a rubber chicken. They made it up just to scare people away. Because ..."

"Because Ghost Island is where the Phoenix Reactor is buried!" yelled Axel.

Agent Omega nodded. "Just a few hours ago I decoded an email from Gus Grabbem Senior himself, the big cheese at Grabbem Industries. Their spies have found out that Doctor Minamoto buried the Phoenix somewhere on – or under – Ghost Island. They're going to try to **steal** it."

"And we need to get to the reactor before Grabbem do," Axel finished. "Got it. You think you can handle this mission, BEAST?"

"I SUPPOSE," said BEAST, without much enthusiasm.

Agent Omega clapped his hands and rubbed them together. "Now we're talking. We'll be at Ghost Island in twenty minutes. Just enough time for me to fit BEAST with a detector that will guide you to the Phoenix Reactor. And there's one other thing, of course."

"What other thing?" asked Axel.

"New apps," said Agent Omega. "Five brand-new forms for you and BEAST to use. And I think you're going to love them."

He pulled a thick cable down from the

MOT-BOL's curved ceiling and plugged it into the back of BEAST's neck. BEAST's eyes went **wobbly** as a flood of data suddenly poured into his system.

"Much quicker to do it this way," said Omega.

As they traveled, Omega explained what the new apps were. **ELASTO** would give BEAST the power to *stretch out* his arms and legs, as if he were made of chewing gum. ("I'm not sure how far BEAST can stretch," warned Omega, "so don't overdo it.") **ARACHNON** was a **spider form**, which could climb up vertical surfaces with ease and shoot web lines to use as grappling ropes or entangle enemies. It would use up much less energy than flying all the time. **SWARMER** was a fast-moving **missile launcher,** capable of firing dozens of micro missiles – "like regular missiles, only smaller"– with pinpoint accuracy. **GALAHAD** was a **fighting form** like OGRE, except GALAHAD equipped one of BEAST's arms with a shield and the other with a sword.

"Isn't that a bit, er, medieval?" Axel asked doubtfully.

"That shield will bounce energy beams right back, and that sword will open up a tank like a can of beans," pointed out Agent Omega. "Now, here's your last app: **BLINKER.** Best not to use this one except in a real emergency. It's highly experimental. Can you guess what it does?"

"Blinks?" Axel guessed.

"Cute. *Blinking* is what Grabbem scientists call **short-range teleporting.** You'll be able to disappear and reappear anywhere within thirty yards."

"Whoa!"

"Impressive, I know. Just don't teleport into anything solid, like a wall. That could be messy."

The hum from the MOT-BOL's engines died down to silence.

"We're here," said Omega. "Welcome to Ghost Island."

Axel climbed back into BEAST and braced himself for whatever would come next.

"I'll hide the Meatball above the clouds," said Agent Omega. "Be careful. Grabbem are probably here already, and they may be expecting you …"

CHAPTER 3

At that very moment, a Grabbem ship was lurking in the fog on the far side of Ghost Island. Axel didn't know it yet, but Agent Omega was right. Grabbem *were* here already.

The ship was long and gray, but it wasn't a battleship. It was broad and flat topped, but it wasn't an aircraft carrier. It was a transporter, and its one job was to transport a colossal robot called **Tektonicus Max.**

The robot covered the entire length of the ship, bow to stern. He lay on his back like a **gigantic zombie** in a tomb, about to arise. A single oval eye looked out from his head. Grabbem technicians fussed over him, checking that all his parts were in working order. This was not as easy as it sounds, because Tektonicus Max – like some toys on Christmas morning – had no batteries at the moment, and none of the technicians were quite sure he would work correctly.

Inside the huge eye – which was in fact a detachable command pod that could pop out and fly around by itself – sat the head of Grabbem Corporation, Mr. Grabbem. He ran his hands over the controls. All the little lights were dark. The buttons clicked, but didn't do anything. **Yet.**

Mr. Grabbem didn't care. He had spent

billions building Tektonicus Max, and many of the Grabbem scientists had whispered to one another that he'd gone **bonkers.** What was the point of a giant robot that had no power source and was so big that no known power source would be enough?

But Mr. Grabbem knew what he was doing. There was a special slot in Tektonicus Max for the Phoenix Reactor to fit into. And when it did ...

"We'll **finish** that brat and his stolen robot once and for all," he grinned. "Stomp him. *Squish!*"

Just then, a roar went up through the abandoned buildings.

Mr. Grabbem turned pale.

"What was that?" he whispered.

The bottom of the Meatball *hissed* open. Axel looked down at Ghost Island, as gray and still as an abandoned battleship, surrounded by banks of fog. From up here, it looked pretty empty. Maybe this mission would be easier than they had thought.

"Let's go," he said.

The Meatball's tentacles released BEAST. They fell down toward the waiting buildings, hurtling through the air, picking up speed as fast as a dropped brick. Axel fired BEAST's foot thrusters to slow them down before they could smash into the ground like a meteorite.

He looked around for a good place to land and spotted an open area that must have been a town square. He landed BEAST on a patch of bare, dry grass in the middle of the buildings and looked around.

The whole place was as still as a graveyard.

They were standing in what must once have been a park, but the trees were all long dead. There wasn't even any wind to stir the ragged flag that hung as limp as a damp towel from a nearby pole. Time had stood still.

"Do you see any sign of Grabbem, BEAST?"

"NOT YET."

"Any radioactive **dragon monsters?**"

"THERE IS RADIATION HERE," warned BEAST. "I AM DETECTING IT NOW. STAY INSIDE YOUR COCKPIT, AXEL. DO NOT LEAVE. DO NOT EVEN OPEN THE DOOR."

BEAST's communicator **crackled.** Agent Omega's voice came through, but it was distorted and kept breaking up. "Axel? – *hiss, pop* – confirm safe landing. There ought to be – *screech, tick-tick-tick* – current location. Can you confirm?"

"Say again?" Axel said. "Didn't catch that."

This time, all that came through the communicator was a squealing, rushing **hiss,** like an old-fashioned radio being tuned. *White noise*, Axel thought.

"RADIATION IS INTERFERING WITH THE SIGNAL," warned BEAST.

"Oh, great! Can you still detect the reactor?"

"YES, BUT NOT VERY CLEARLY. IT WILL HELP IF WE CAN SCAN FROM SEVERAL DIFFERENT LOCATIONS. AND AXEL, I THINK WE SHOULD HURRY. SOMETHING IS WRONG."

"Yeah. I'm with you. Let's find that reactor and get out of here."

BEAST marked three points he wanted to scan from, on top of three different buildings. Axel shifted BEAST into ARACHNON form.

He felt a little **peculiar** to see BEAST's arms and legs split neatly in two, then extend out into **spidery limbs** with pincers on the end.

ARACHNON **scuttled** across the square and up the side of the nearest office building. Axel didn't want to look into the windows as they climbed, but he couldn't stop himself. In one room he saw a toppled-over chair beside a desk, as if the office worker had run away in terror. The desk had a cup of ancient coffee on it, thick with mold.

It might not have been ghosts, he thought, *but SOMETHING scared these people away. What could it have been?*

Then, from somewhere nearby, a groaning roar ripped through the air.

It was a roar filled with **rage** and **hunger.** It sounded like no animal of this

Earth. An unknown dinosaur might bellow like that, perhaps – a forgotten king of the dinosaurs, huger than anything before or since, thankfully lost to history. It was a roar to make anything warm-blooded **run and hide.**

BEAST clamped himself to the wall and huddled there. Axel froze on the spot, chilled to the bone. "What was that?"

"BEAST DOES NOT KNOW!"

"Machinery? Something from an old industrial plant? **A rusty crane turning in the wind?** Tell me that's what it was!"

"THERE IS NO WIND," said BEAST, sounding small and terrified.

Axel glanced down into the streets. He couldn't see anything, but some deep instinct told him the streets weren't as empty as they looked.

He said, "Chances are it's a Grabbem machine of some kind. Get your scan done, quick. We need to move."

Once BEAST's first scan was done, Axel used the ARACHNON web projector to launch a web line across the street to the building opposite. The cable **latched** on, and BEAST clambered out and across.

"This way we can stay up on the rooftops, out of the streets," explained Axel.

"THAT IS FINE BY ME!" said BEAST.

Once they reached the building, ARACHNON's spidery legs **scrambled** easily over the walls and ledges to get to their target. Soon they were ready for their second scan.

Axel felt **sweaty** and **nervous,** and the controls were **slippery** in his hands. What if the terrible noise happened again?

The next second, it did happen again, and closer. The **roar** was so loud the building vibrated. The glass in the windowpanes shook and one of the panes shattered.

He looked around to see where the roar had come from. Still there was nothing.

Then he saw something that made him feel like he'd missed a step going downstairs and had fallen **helpless** and **headlong** into a nightmare. An abandoned car down in the streets – a car he could have sworn was undamaged seconds before – was crushed flat.

Just as if some colossal, invisible monster had stomped down on it, he thought.

"How's that scan coming, BEAST?"

"ALL DONE."

"One more to go. Then we grab that reactor and we get out of here."

The last scanning point was halfway up a metal radio mast. ARACHNON had no trouble climbing up it. He looked like a huge house spider **scrambling** up the screen on a window.

As the antennae on ARACHNON's bulbous head began to twitch and swivel, scanning for the Phoenix Reactor, Axel watched the street below.

Whatever's out there, it knows we're scanning. It wants to scare us off. This HAS to be a Grabbem trick. Well, BEAST and I don't scare easy!

"AXEL, I WANT YOU TO KNOW THAT I AM **VERY SCARED**," said BEAST.

"Remember what Agent Omega said, BEAST. There's no monster here. It's just a story that someone made up to scare people. But Grabbem are real –"

A tremendously powerful *something* smashed into the radio mast below them. BEAST let out an electronic **squeal** as the mast buckled and began to collapse.

Axel's reflexes went into overdrive. He grabbed the aiming control, locked the web projector on to the nearest surface he could find – a huge billboard **– and fired.**

ARACHNON's web line shot out toward the billboard, which showed a smiling woman holding a dish full of noodles. The web line *thunked* into her left nostril and stuck fast.

Axel punched the control to reel them in.

ARACHNON whizzed up the web line, away from the toppling radio mast, and ended up dangling from the smiling woman's nose like a **massive spider-shaped ...**

The mast crashed down into the street. Clouds of dust swirled in the air where the mast's base had been torn up from the ground. The dust clung to the thing that they hadn't been able to see before.

The thing that had crushed the car.

The thing that had roared.

Axel felt the blood drain from his face.

"THE GHOST ISLAND MONSTER!" said BEAST. "IT'S REAL!"

CHAPTER 4

Axel could barely see the "monster." The dust clung to its invisible body in patches, making it look ghostly and half-real. He saw lumbering legs, **a claw,** a swaying dinosaur-like head. It was looking back and forth along the empty streets, searching for something. For them, no doubt.

Axel punched the communicator button. "Agent Omega? We're going to need that evac.

We have a very big problem down here!"

All that came through the speakers was a nasty hissing buzz, like someone making a **wasp smoothie** in a kitchen blender.

"He can't hear us," Axel said. "We're on our own."

"CAN WE JUST STAY HANGING HERE?" BEAST said. "BEAST DOES NOT MIND. BEAST IS ACTUALLY QUITE COMFORTABLE."

"I wish we could," said Axel. "But we need to beat Grabbem to the Phoenix Reactor. This is probably some kind of trick of theirs to scare us off."

A rhythmic **boom, boom, boom** told them the thing was on the move again. It left deep footprints. Right before his eyes, Axel saw a car crushed to a flat mat of metal as the monster stomped on it.

"I HAVE A LOCK ON THE REACTOR," said BEAST.

Axel glanced at BEAST's map and saw that the blinking signal was just where he feared it would be – on the other side of the monster. They'd have to get past it to reach their goal.

The monster stopped in its tracks. Its half-visible head turned to face BEAST. It hesitated. Then it reached up a claw and tugged something in its shoulder. It must have been a switch, because the next moment its whole body shimmered and it steadily became clearly visible, like a **demon** taking physical form.

It's done playing games, Axel thought. *No more hiding. It wants to fight.*

Crimson and black **armor plating** came slowly into view. The monster's metal breastplate was battered, as if from countless battles.

"IT IS NOT A MONSTER! IT IS A ROBOT!" gasped BEAST. **"LIKE ME!"**

BEAST was right. The "monster" was made of mechanical parts. The tail was a segmented, intricate creation, the eyes were glowing lenses, and the claws were **hydraulic pincers.**

"It's a Grabbem attack bot," Axel said. "I knew it!"

It'd be just like Grabbem to build a super-mean robot after they accidentally built a kind and gentle one like BEAST, Axel thought.

With a sound of grinding gears, the attack bot's mouth opened. A **red lance** of fiery light blazed from between its jaws.

BEAST **squealed in panic** and Axel grabbed his controls, thinking, *We're dead. I was too slow. I should have seen that coming.*

But the attack bot's blast didn't hit BEAST head-on. It tore through the ARACHNON web line, blackening and splitting it like burned spaghetti and turning the noodle woman's face into a **smoldering** crater.

The cable snapped and ARACHNON fell.

Axel tried to aim and fire another web line, but he was seconds too slow. ARACHNON dropped with a mighty crash and lay twitching on its back, looking a lot like a real spider that had been swatted down from the ceiling. Axel was slammed around inside BEAST's cockpit. **"Ow!"** he yelled.

The attack bot reared back its head and a new sound came from its gaping jaws. It was an ugly, stop-start kind of a sound, but that wasn't what made it horrible.

It was a *laugh.*

Axel narrowed his eyes. Memories came back to him. He'd been laughed at before, back in school, when the bullies had ganged up on him in packs. In those days, nobody had been on his side. He hadn't had BEAST then. But now he did, and things were different.

"Shift form," he snarled. **"Go into GALAHAD."**

"SHIFTING!" said BEAST, who – Axel was glad to hear – also sounded more angry than hurt.

In a single flip, ARACHNON rolled over and crouched down among the rubble. Its eight limbs folded back into four.

BEAST's legs thickened and grew tall. From his left arm, a metal shield inflated like a life raft, locking into place with a steely *snap*. Its surface was mirror bright. From his right hand a long blade extended. Axel had expected it to look like steel, too, but it was some sort of transparent material like diamond. *A crystal*

sword that can cut through a tank, he thought dizzily.

BEAST's head was the last to change. The bug-like ARACHNON head vanished in a blur of shifting parts. In its place was an armored bump with eyes in it, **like an iron potato.**

Axel nodded with grim satisfaction. He heaved GALAHAD out of the crater where they had fallen and stomped down the street to face the ghostly robot.

It was still there, though difficult to see. Only a hundred yards away from them, it tilted its head and watched with interest as they strode toward it. For the first time, Axel saw its tail moving behind it, **thrashing** back and forth.

"Hey, you! Want to try that blaster of yours again?" Axel yelled.

The robot let out a mean-sounding **_hiss._** Its jaws flew open.

Axel quickly brought up the shield and then fell to one knee so it would cover GALAHAD's entire body.

The robot's red blast lashed into GALAHAD's shield, which thrummed like a guitar string as it took the impact. To the robot's clear surprise, the shield didn't just look like a mirror, it worked like one, too. The blast rebounded off at an angle, punching right through a ground-floor shop and out the other side, pulverizing an abandoned gas station in the next street.

Axel and the attack bot both looked at the **massive hole in the building**, and then looked at each other.

The two robots faced one another in the abandoned street.

"BAKA," the attack bot said, in a deep voice that seemed to purr with hate.

"TRANSLATING," said BEAST. "THE WORD *BAKA* MEANS – "

"I know what it means," interrupted Axel. He didn't speak Japanese, but he had been on the Internet often enough to learn a few things.

Baka was a very common insult in Japan. It meant "fool."

"We'll see who's the *baka* here, you Grabbem scrap pile," he whispered.

He drew back GALAHAD's sword arm, ready to strike, crouching low, and carefully kept the shield up in case the attack bot tried that blast beam again. Then he jerked

GALAHAD's head backward twice, sending a message that he was sure the attack bot would understand. It was the universal gesture for **come at me, bro.**

The attack bot bellowed in fury. It lowered its head and charged.

CHAPTER 5

Axel stood his ground as the attack bot thundered toward him.

One good, hard sword blow should stop it in its tracks. He just had to keep his nerve until it got close enough.

He knew exactly where he'd strike. Just above the attack bot's left hip was a mass of exposed cables. BEAST's enhanced vision labeled them as **unarmored.** The crystal blade should slice through them like soft macaroni.

The robot grinned. It bore down on him, claws outstretched. It almost seemed to be daring Axel to attack it, as if this were a game of chicken.

Axel held his breath. Closer … closer … almost there. He could feel the vibrations of the thing's pounding feet.

He swung – and the attack bot *leapt*, as if it had known the blow was coming. It soared up into the air – GALAHAD's sword blade swished harmlessly beneath – and then down it came, **Plunging** toward the spot where Axel stood.

The world seemed to go into slow motion. In half a second, that thing was going to hit him with the force of a ten-ton truck falling off a cliff. The shield wouldn't help. He needed to move!

He dived forward, away from the plummeting nightmare.

THOOOM. The attack bot landed behind them.

Axel rolled head over heels and stood up, unsteadily.

The attack bot spun around to face them.

Axel spun around, too. He turned the movement into a **sword slash** and aimed the blade at the enemy robot's neck.

Startled, the attack bot tried to ward off the sword blow with its claws.

Snikt! The blade sheared clean through one of the razor-sharp talons. The talon fell to the ground with a clatter.

Axel felt suddenly guilty, as if he'd kicked a football through a window and now he'd have to pay for it.

While the maimed attack bot stared at its stump of a talon and roared, Axel got into a combat stance.

The attack bot charged at him. This time, it had none of the gloating patience it had shown before. **Now, it was mad.**

It lunged at GALAHAD with a flurry of claw rakes that bounced harmlessly off the shield. The jaws **snapped,** biting at GALAHAD's face.

Axel brought the shield up for protection, and the attack bot's jaws closed on its edge. It hung there, its jaws locked, like a dog that won't let go of a Frisbee, until Axel began to wonder if it was trying to chew the shield to pieces.

"Get off!" he yelled. He tried to hit it with the sword again, but the attack bot caught GALAHAD's thick wrist with its clawed hand and held it fast. Now both of BEAST's arms were pinned, one by the jaws and one by the claws.

Growling, the attack bot forced them backward until they were pressed up against a brick wall.

"WARNING. MY INTERNAL SYSTEMS ARE BEING CRUSHED," said BEAST.

"Can you shift?"

"IMPOSSIBLE. I CANNOT RETRACT MY ARMS!"

A cold feeling of horror ran through Axel then. Did this vicious robot *know* about BEAST's shifting ability? Was it doing this on purpose?

"I said **get off,**" he snarled.

He tilted GALAHAD's head back and then slammed it suddenly into the attack bot's own face, **in a mighty head-butt.**

The attack bot let go and went staggering back, stunned.

Axel smiled a grim little smile. Even when you had no weapons left to fight with, you still had yourself.

As the attack bot **tottered** unsteadily in front of him, Axel lifted the sword for a final finishing blow.

Then, before his astonished eyes, the attack bot began to *shift*, just like BEAST could. It hunched over, and from its back came thick armor plates that snapped into place. They formed a domed shell, covering its back and neck completely. The dinosaur-like head morphed into a stubby little head with a curved beak – *like a turtle,* Axel thought. Finally, the thin whiplike tail thickened into a heavy club-tipped tail.

"It's not just a robot, it's a **shifter!**" Axel said in amazement.

His sword was still raised for the final blow. He brought the sword down on the turtle robot as hard as he could.

With a deafening *shrangggg* that sent numbing vibrations up his arm, the crystal sword rebounded off the shell.

"We didn't even **scratch** it!" Axel moaned.

The turtle robot pawed at the ground with clawed feet that were now wide and flat. The next moment it lunged, **gnashing** at BEAST's neck with its metal beak.

Axel swiped wildly at it, but the crystal blade hit the shell and bounced off once again.

The huge hooked jaws locked around BEAST's neck, and steadily began to close ...

CHAPTER 6

At that very moment, a Grabbem sky fighter was circling above Ghost Island.

The sky fighter was ugly and roughly triangular. If you imagine a broad slice of **pizza** made from metal with a **golf ball** squished into the middle of it, only the golf ball is made of armored glass, then you'll have a pretty good idea of what it looked like.

Dangling from the underside of the sky fighter were a lot of bombs. They were knobbly and spiky and had big, clear warning labels on them, like **DANGER! BOMB!** and **CONTENTS MAY EXPLODE!** and **DO NOT HIT WITH HAMMER!**

If you were wondering what sort of person would be silly enough to look at a bomb and think, *Hmm, I wonder what would happen if I hit this bomb with a hammer* in the first place, then you could have taken a look into the armored glass ball and seen exactly that kind of person. Two of them, in fact.

They were Grabbem employees: brothers, code-named Alpha One and Alpha Gold. For this mission, Alpha One had wanted to call himself **Alpha Battle Werewolf Storm Titan Warrior With A Bigger Gun Than You,** but Grabbem Command had told him he had better stop with all the name change requests because he was on one formal warning already, and besides it wouldn't fit on his name tag.

Alpha One was in the top half of the glass ball, working the flight controls. He had a huge grin on his face.

Alpha Gold was in the bottom half. He would have been working the fighter's weapons if there had been anything to **shoot at** or **blow up,** but there wasn't. He had his arms folded and his bottom lip stuck out.

"It's my turn to fly the ship," he whined.

"You've been flying in circles for hours!"

"Ah, be quiet," snapped Alpha One. "I'm on controls; you're on weapons. That was the deal."

"It isn't fair. We're meant to be keeping watch while the guys on the ground grab the reactor, but there's been nobody to **shoot** at. I'm bored."

"Too bad! We made a deal. You can't go back on it now." Alpha One weaved the ship in a quick turn just so Alpha Gold would get thrown around in his half of the bubble.

"Hey! Knock it off! I'm going to throw up!"

"You can always hit that **eee-ject** button if you don't like the ride," grinned Alpha One.

Alpha Gold stood up in his seat, reached through the hatch between the cockpits and tried to grab Alpha One's leg so he could pull him out of his chair. Alpha One quickly put his feet up on his dashboard.

"Too slow!" he crowed.

Just as Alpha Gold was about to force his way into Alpha One's cockpit and punch him in the face, an alert went off. He quickly dropped back down into his own cockpit and checked the screens.

"Hostile targets ahead," he said, his eyes wide.

"What?" his brother boggled. "This place is meant to be dead. There aren't any hostiles. You're reading it wrong."

"See for yourself!" yelled Alpha Gold.

Sure enough, there were two red glowing shapes on the console. The view auto-zoomed in to show they were BEAST, still in GALAHAD form, and the robotic turtle monster, locked in a **deadly grapple.**

"Well, I'll be **whang-doodled,"**

gasped Alpha One, shaking his head. "It's that kid who keeps on giving us the runaround. And some other robot critter, too."

Alpha Gold rubbed his hands together. "Woo-hoo! Bring us in close. I'm going to bomb the pair of them to kingdom come!" He pressed a row of buttons. The clamps holding the bombs in place unlocked so they could be dropped.

"No way," yelled Alpha One. He unfastened his safety harness and leaned down through the hatch. "You fly the ship. It's your turn. *I'm* going to **drop the bombs.**"

"Get back in that seat NOW!" hollered Alpha Gold. "You said it yourself. We had a deal!"

"You wanted to fly the ship, so YOU fly the ship!" screamed Alpha One. He lowered himself into Alpha Gold's half and landed on top of him.

The two of them fought over the weapons controls, elbowing each other and shouting and paying no attention to the way their craft was steadily dropping farther and farther down. The sky fighter was plunging right toward the skyline of the city.

Meanwhile, down in the abandoned streets, Axel struggled with the **turtle robot.** Its grip on BEAST's neck was growing tighter. If he couldn't stop it, it would **bite** right through. Somehow he doubted that the MOT-BOL could put BEAST's head back on if it came off.

The turtle form seemed much stronger than the dinosaur-like one, though it was slower. *It traded speed for strength,* Axel thought giddily. *It has to lose something to gain something. Just like BEAST does when he shifts form ...*

Just then, he caught sight of something like a huge slice of metallic pizza in the sky. It was hurtling toward them as if it meant to attack. From the G symbols on the wings, there was no doubt who it belonged to.

The turtle robot saw it, too. It hesitated for a second, then let go of BEAST. Its eyes flared a brilliant red. Two beams of dazzling light shot from them – *right at the Grabbem ship!*

The ship lurched to the side and the beams missed.

With a snarl, the attack bot turned back to Axel.

"Wait, wait! You shot at them?" Axel said, amazed. **"I thought you were with Grabbem!"**

A hesitant voice came from the turtle robot's chest. It said: "You mean ... you're *not* with Grabbem?"

"Grabbem hates us. They're hunting us. Because we keep spoiling their plans!"

"Oh," said the voice. "I see."

Just like that, the fight was over.

Axel and the turtle robot stepped away from one another, **completely confused**, and more than a little awkward.

"Why didn't you say something sooner?" Axel said.

"You're trespassing," said the turtle robot. "And you attacked me."

"You shot us!"

"I shot your cable. I didn't shoot you! But you ... you swung that sword at me. You *challenged* me. You expect me to just stand there and take it?"

BEAST said, "I AM SORRY TO INTERRUPT, BUT I BELIEVE WE ARE ALL ABOUT TO DIE."

"What?" gasped Axel.

"MULTIPLE BOMBS INCOMING."

Axel couldn't have known it, but up in the Grabbem ship, Alpha One had accidentally stomped on all the bomb-dropping switches at once. Alpha One didn't notice – he was too busy trying to bite Alpha Gold's ear, while Alpha Gold pulled One's underpants up and gave him a **death wedgie.**

As the two of them fought and the attack ship spun out of control, an entire payload of bombs went tumbling down toward the two robots.

The last thing Axel saw before the bombs hit was the **turtle robot** leaping at him and grabbing hold of BEAST. Then there was a sound like the whole world shattering to pieces – and everything went dark.

CHAPTER 7

At that very moment, in a cavern deep below the derelict city, a squad of ten handpicked Grabbem combat operatives were aiming their rifles and holding their breath.

They were aiming at a circular steel vault door with the symbol of a phoenix on it.

A single Grabbem agent was cutting his way through it with a laser torch, **very, very slowly.**

Mr. Grabbem hovered above them, sitting inside the giant detached eye of Tektonicus Max. "Can't he cut any faster?" he yelled at the men. **"I want that reactor NOW!"**

The men's commander, Captain Weiss – who looked like he punched people in the face with *his* face – roared at the man with the laser torch: "Do you have a Code 9 booboo in your standard issue wumpus, soldier? Do you want to be busted back to Dixie Foxtrot Corndog?"

"No sir!" wailed the man. He had no clue what Captain Weiss was talking about, because Captain Weiss only ever yelled **military-sounding gibberish.** Everyone pretended to understand, but it sounded scary.

"Then do your job, you **chicken gizzard!**"

Sweat ran from the man's forehead. His hands shook as he tried to go faster.

Almost there ...

Axel was falling.

He had only a moment to wonder how that could be, since he'd been standing on solid ground a moment ago. And then suddenly he wasn't falling anymore.

CRASH! GALAHAD slammed down on a hard, rocky surface. There was a second **CRASH** as the other robot fell close by.

From overhead came the ***boom, boom, kaboom*** of the Grabbem bombs pounding the empty city.

Axel tried to sit up, but GALAHAD's heavy armor made it difficult. He shifted

BEAST back into his regular form. Somehow he didn't think the other robot was much of a threat anymore.

They had fallen down into a darkened cavern. High above them was a jagged hole, where the bombs had blasted right through the sidewalk.

"The bombs must have blown us into the mines under the island," he said. "Look at the size of the hole they made! I don't understand why **we're still alive.**"

BEAST said, "WE WERE **SHIELDED** FROM THE BLAST."

Axel looked at the turtle robot, who was struggling to stand, and he understood. He went and helped the robot to its feet.

Instantly it *shifted*. Its shell folded away, its limbs extended and its head took on a shape like a motorcycle helmet. The next second, a black and red robot was standing in front of them. It looked so much like BEAST that the two might have been cousins.

"Thanks," said Axel. "You used your shell to protect us, didn't you?"

The robot nodded.

"I'm Axel," said Axel. "This is BEAST. Thank you for saving our lives."

"You needn't thank me. It's my job to protect **foolish people** from doing harm to themselves or others," said a voice from inside the robot.

Axel's cheeks flushed hot.

The robot's chest opened up. Inside, giving him a calculating look, was a girl. She climbed out of her robot and stood beside it. Axel wasn't sure what to do, so he climbed out of BEAST, too.

Axel swallowed. "I'm Axel," he said.

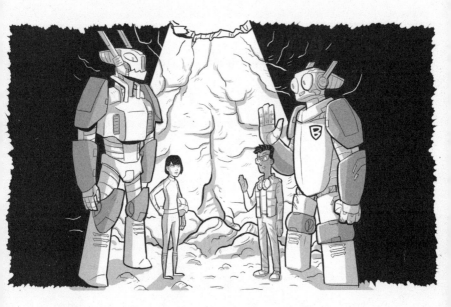

"And, uh, this is BEAST."

"Yumi Minamoto," the girl said. "And my robot, who you have damaged, is REAVER."

"I AM VERY, VERY SORRY MY PILOT MADE ME HIT YOU, REAVER," said BEAST. "YOU ARE AN INCREDIBLE ROBOT. YOUR DESIGN IS AMAZING. YOUR SPEED IS PHENOMENAL. YOUR

ABILITIES ARE –"

"BE QUIET," said a deep, growling, electronic voice. Axel recognized it. It was the one that had said *baka* earlier on. It must be REAVER'S own voice.

"REAVER!" snapped Yumi. "Don't be rude."

"APOLOGIES. I FIND IT HARD TO BE POLITE TO ONE SO ... **INFERIOR.**" The robot's eyes flickered red as he spoke. Axel felt BEAST cringe.

"Yumi-san," he said quickly, "I have a *lot* of questions."

"One moment. While we were busy fighting one another because we each thought the other was with Grabbem, the real Grabbem team must have snuck down here ahead of us."

"You're right. They might even have found the reactor by now!"

"REAVER? Go into RATATRON form. Dig us a passage down to the vault," said Yumi.

REAVER shifted into a new form, a sleek ratlike creature. Instead of whiskers, dim beams of laser light shone from its muzzle. He **bounded** off into the dark, leaving BEAST gazing after him.

"SHALL I GO INTO GOPHER FORM?" BEAST asked Axel eagerly.

"It's not loaded, but good idea. See if he needs any help anyway."

REAVER's voice grated out from the shadows: "I DO NOT NEED HELP!" But BEAST was already **lolloping** after him.

"I think your robot has a crush on my robot," murmured Yumi. "That's adorable."

Left alone with Yumi, Axel suddenly felt awkward and out of his depth. Fighting was easy compared to having to socialize.

Pull yourself together, he told himself. *Agent Omega is counting on you. We need that reactor.*

He coughed. "Did you say your family name was Minamoto?"

"That's right. And I bet I know what you're going to say next."

"Let's see if I can put this together," said Axel. "You're the daughter of Doctor Minamoto, who designed the Phoenix Reactor."

"Correct."

"Which is buried somewhere underneath this island."

"Also correct. Sealed in a steel vault, to be precise."

"And you and REAVER have been guarding it. Putting out stories about how the place is haunted by a monster. I bet you even created the radiation somehow."

"Of course I did," said Yumi. "Anyone could have worked that out. Now I have a question for you. Think carefully. How come your robot can shift, like mine?"

Axel shook his head. "You've got it the wrong way around. *Your* robot can shift, like *mine*."

Yumi laughed. "You think those lunkheads at Grabbem came up with shifter technology all by themselves? *Think*, Axel! Grabbem don't create, they *take*. They **stole the secrets** to creating shifters from us. REAVER was the first shifter ever to be built! And he was designed by –"

"Your mother," Axel interrupted. "Doctor Minamoto."

Yumi gave him a searching look. "Good guess."

"I had a hunch."

"She built REAVER for me. The most advanced robot of his kind. Your BEAST is merely an imitation."

"I get it!" Axel snapped. "REAVER's cool. But BEAST's cool, too. So what if he's not the original? He can't help how he was created, so leave him alone!"

"Are you this fiercely loyal to all your friends?" Yumi said with a grin. But her smile faded when she saw the look on Axel's face. "Oh. You do *have* friends other than BEAST … right?"

"A charming guy like me?" said Axel sarcastically. "Oh, yeah. More friends than I can count. I mean, we've only just met, and look how well *we're* getting along!"

From across the cavern came BEAST's happy yell: **"WE HAVE DUG YOU A PASSAGE!"**

Axel and Yumi looked at each other. At exactly the same time, they both said, "Let's go."

CHAPTER 8

Axel and Yumi clambered down the freshly dug tunnel. They were back inside their robots now. Both BEAST and REAVER were in their regular forms, so they could quickly shift into whatever new form might be needed.

Axel saw a **flashing** dot on his scanner.

"The reactor's only a few hundred yards in front of us," he whispered over the radio.

"Yeah. Exactly where I left it," said Yumi. "That's good news. It means Grabbem haven't stolen it yet. We might still be in time to stop them."

At its end, the tunnel widened out into a cavern. Flickering light came from up ahead: the light of a **laser torch** in action.

Moving as quietly as they could, Axel and Yumi crept into the cavern.

They soon saw they were standing right behind a group of Grabbem soldiers. The detached eye of Tektonicus Max hovered above, shining a beam of light at the vault.

The soldiers hadn't noticed Axel and Yumi. They were all facing the vault door, where one **frightened** Grabbem soldier was cutting his way through, watched over by a scowling Captain Weiss.

"We got here just in time. Looks like they're

almost through," Yumi said.

"And there's Mr. Grabbem himself, in that hovering eye thing!" Axel glanced around in case his son, Gus Grabbem Junior, was lurking somewhere. No sign. Maybe the **repulsive** boy had been grounded for once.

"We've got about sixty seconds to come up with a plan," said Yumi.

Axel swallowed and forced himself to think. "Okay. How about this? The moment they open the vault, I'll use BEAST's ELASTO form to stretch out and grab the reactor."

Yumi nodded. "And I can use REAVER's LIGHTRAZOR form to keep the guards off your back."

"LIGHTRAZOR?"

"It's his superfast energy attack mode," said Yumi.

"Cool. It'll be like a **combo blitz move.**"

"Totally."

Axel laughed. "Did we just come up with a plan?"

"Yup. With thirty seconds to spare, too."

Axel held up BEAST's fist. Yumi made REAVER give him a **fist bump.**

For the first time on this mission, Axel suddenly felt really deep-down good. He'd never guessed there were people other than him and Omega fighting Grabbem – people he could fight alongside, and even learn from. *Maybe I'm not alone after all,* he thought.

"BEAST, go into ELASTO!"

BEAST changed shape into something like an orangutan with long, droopy, springlike limbs. Across from them, REAVER had gone into LIGHTRAZOR, which looked like a sleek, athletic alien with softly glowing blades for arms. By comparison, BEAST looked

ridiculous, but he clearly didn't care. He was having the time of his life.

The Grabbem agent with the torch leapt backward. A thick disk of metal with smoldering edges toppled out and fell with a crash that echoed throughout the cavern.

An unearthly light – crimson and gold like a sunset – blazed out from inside the vault. All the agents gasped at once. Axel could just make out the light's source: a cylinder that looked like a lava lamp, thrumming with power.

"The Phoenix Reactor," said Mr. Grabbem, licking his lips. "Come to Daddy!" His eye-craft drifted forward.

"Axel, **quick,** grab it before he does!" yelled Yumi.

Axel went into action. Leaving his legs locked in place, BEAST reached out with his arms and shot forward and up with a steely **sproinnnggg,** extending out like a stretchy piece of gum. He arched right over the astonished Grabbem guards, **a robotic rainbow.**

"It's that kid again," roared Mr. Grabbem. **"Ooh, he's the biggest pain in the world!** Well? Don't just stand around, you **useless lumps.** Stop him!"

Captain Weiss tilted the top of his head back like a pez dispenser and screamed, "You heard the man! **Bogey Dingo Niner** on a quad bike, go, go, go!"

The guards swiveled their rifles around and pointed them at BEAST. But before they could fire, REAVER rushed out of the shadows as quick and silent as a pouncing panther. He zipped all the way down the line of guards and with one **slash** of his arm, he sliced right through their rifle barrels as easily as if he'd been cutting through bamboo. He skidded to a halt and turned around in one graceful motion.

The rifle barrels fell **clinkety-clank** to the ground like useless lengths of plumbing. The guards stared at the stumps of their

weapons, unable to understand what had just happened.

Axel kept on stretching above their heads. He hoped BEAST would be able to stretch far enough. The longer his body got, the thinner it got. It was getting pretty cramped inside BEAST's cockpit. BEAST's arms

couldn't stretch any farther, so he stretched his fingers instead. They reached for the Phoenix Reactor. Almost ... almost ... **got it!**

Captain Weiss took out a big, ugly handgun and took aim. "Tic-tacs on my poodle, hunky dunker," he snarled. "Going to banjax your Ralphie Tango all the way to South Central!"

"What?" said Axel.

Weiss opened fire. BEAST catapulted his body backward, like elastic twanging back, and the bullets **pinged** harmlessly off the cavern wall. BEAST's torso wobbled giddily around. His eyes rolled around in his head. But he kept a tight grip on the Phoenix Reactor.

"Good work," Yumi called across to him. "Now let's get out of here."

Axel shifted BEAST back into his usual

form, glad to be done with ELASTO. That form had been useful, but all the *boinging* around made you feel seasick.

He turned and ran back up the tunnel. REAVER came racing up to join them, and together they headed toward the surface. Captain Weiss fired wildly at REAVER, but the elegant robot ducked and weaved out of the way with hardly any effort at all.

"Oh no. We're not having that," said Gus Grabbem. He shoved the levers forward in his eye-craft and went zooming up the tunnel like a bowling ball in a gutter.

Axel and Yumi glanced back over their shoulders and saw him looming up behind them.

REAVER sprinted on ahead, but BEAST saw Mr. Grabbem's furious face and let out a tiny, terrified squeak. He staggered.

"BEAST, run!" Axel yelled.

BEAST recovered himself. He put on a burst of speed. Mr. Grabbem was already catching up. He pressed a button. A thin telescopic arm with clutching fingers emerged from under the eye.

From up ahead, REAVER hissed angrily: **"THROW ME THE PHOENIX REACTOR, YOU FOOL. I AM FASTER THAN YOU."**

Before either Axel or Yumi could say anything, BEAST – eager to please – had hurled the Phoenix Reactor toward REAVER.

It spun through the air, end over end, **lighting up the tunnel** with its intense glow.

REAVER went in for the catch, but Mr. Grabbem's **telescopic arm** shot forward with blinding speed and snatched the reactor out of the air. It vanished inside his craft.

Grabbem **guffawed.** "Thanks. That was easier than I expected."

The guards were pouring into the tunnel, and they had replaced their sliced-off rifles with scary-looking new weapons. Axel saw rocket launchers, grenades and something that looked like a mini gun.

"Now what?" Axel yelled.

"We take him down," Yumi said, her voice shaking with anger.

Mr. Grabbem reversed away from them, crowing over his prize. One of the guards tossed a fist-sized *something* past him into the tunnel.

"Bye-bye, **kiddiewinks,**" said Grabbem.

A red light blinked on the object for a second.

"Grenade!" shouted Yumi.

Axel went staggering back as the grenade exploded. The tunnel filled with tumbling rubble and choking dust.

When it had cleared enough to see, they saw the tunnel was blocked from floor to ceiling. There was no way through to catch Mr. Grabbem now.

CHAPTER 9

"No time for blame. We need to get to the surface, **fast,**" Yumi said.

BEAST fired his foot thrusters and REAVER sprang forward like a grasshopper. They reached the ragged-walled shaft where the bombs had blasted them down into the mine tunnels.

With BEAST flying and REAVER hopping from surface to surface before it could crumble under his weight, they quickly made it back up into the open.

"There he goes!" Axel pointed to where Mr. Grabbem's eye-craft was zooming out to sea, toward the huge shape of a ship, half-visible in the sea mist. There was something else there, something on top of the ship ... but, no, it couldn't be. A robot the height of a high-rise, lying on its back?

"REAVER," stammered BEAST. "I AM SORRY. WE FAILED AND IT IS MY FAULT."

REAVER snorted a **"HA!"** but Yumi spoke over him: "You have nothing to apologize for, BEAST."

BEAST and REAVER both said, **"WHAT?"**

"Through this entire mission, you have clearly done your best. REAVER, on the other hand, has been a fool. It is he who should apologize to you."

"APOLOGIZE?" grated REAVER as if he'd been told to sit up and beg like a good puppy.

"Yes! BEAST was doing fine until you told him to throw the reactor to you, just so you could show off how much better than him you think you are! And because he wanted to impress you, he did as he was told. Do you think you are in charge here?"

"NO," said REAVER softly. **"BUT I UNDERSTAND NOW."**

"And?"

"I AM SORRY, BEAST."

"OKAY!" said Beast happily. "I AM GLAD WE ARE FRIENDS AGAIN."

REAVER's eyes flashed red, but he said nothing.

Axel said, "Guys ... I think Grabbem's coming back."

"In that floating eye?"

"Not exactly. You'd better look and see for yourself."

A colossal figure was striding toward them through the sea. It was so tall that waves washed against its shins. The high-rise buildings of Ghost Island only came up to its chest. It turned its huge helmetlike head back and forth, with a grinding noise like a ship's anchor chain **swinging.** In the middle of its forehead was a single huge eye, and looking out from the eyeball's lens was Mr. Grabbem.

"Hey, kid!" came his voice, massively amplified, ringing out between the empty buildings. "Glad we caught up! What do you think of **my** robot suit, eh?"

"Boys and their toys," Yumi said with a half smile. "It's all about who's got the big expensive one."

"You about ready to get **stomped flat?**" Grabbem yelled.

"It's me he's after," Axel said. "You should get out of here."

Yumi gave him a withering look. "**Please.** I'm here to get my property back. And I'm not leaving without it."

Tektonicus Max came stomping up the shore. The ground **shook** and **wobbled** like a backyard trampoline under its feet. It looked at a building, seemed to ponder something for a moment, and then casually swatted it with its fist. The building came crashing down in a shower of rubble, as if it had been a sandcastle kicked over on the beach. The rubble turned to **glowing dust** and faded away.

"THAT IS A VERY POWERFUL ROBOT," said BEAST.

"It's not even our biggest problem," Yumi said. "That Grabbem fool doesn't realize the Phoenix Reactor is *unstable*. If we don't pull it out of his robot and shut it down, it'll destroy everything within a hundred miles of here."

"So we fight," said Axel.

"Agreed," said Yumi.

"AGREED," said REAVER.

"AGREED," said BEAST.

Tektonicus Max stomped up the street toward them. He punched down entire office buildings as he came. The masonry turned into glittering nothingness as fast as it came **crashing** down.

"Time for another one of our famous thirty-second plans?" said Axel.

Yumi nodded. "I'll shift REAVER into his black widow form, DARKWEAVER. He can spin polymer webs that even that *mecha* won't be able to break. Can you keep Grabbem busy with some kind of hit-and-run attack?"

"The SWARMER form should be good for that," said Axel.

"Cool. Get him to chase you. I'll trip him with a web line, then quickly tie him down. Once he's immobile, you pull the reactor out."

The two robots shifted form. SWARMER had caterpillar tracks to **ZOOM** around on, while both BEAST's arms turned into stubby missile launchers. DARKWEAVER was a lot like ARACHNON, but lean and gleaming black. He went scuttling off into the shadows by the side of the road. SWARMER took up position in the open, where Grabbem would be sure to see him.

And see him he did. "Hold still! This won't take a second!" boomed Mr. Grabbem.

Tektonicus Max came bounding down the road with huge earthshaking strides.

Axel lined up the aiming crosshairs and fired. Missiles streaked toward Tektonicus Max in a flaming cloud, like fireworks going off. They blew up in its face, fountaining fire and sparks everywhere.

The gigantic robot staggered, and for a second Axel thought, *We got him. He's going down already. It must have been a lucky shot.* But then he heard Mr. Grabbem laughing.

"Is that all you've got? Those **poxy little shots?** Didn't even leave a scratch!"

Axel reversed SWARMER up the road, acting like he was trying to keep Tektonicus Max at a distance. He fired again, but Tektonicus Max **swatted** the micro missiles out of the air, just like a man irritably shooing a fly from his drink. DARKWEAVER crouched just ahead of him, still hidden, waiting for the moment.

"Wait till my son hears I was the one who dealt with you," leered Mr. Grabbem. "He'll be so jealous!"

"You've not dealt with me yet," yelled Axel.

"Oh, I will. Just watch!"

Tektonicus Max lurched forward again. The mighty metal foot came down – and DARKWEAVER whizzed across its path, a **blur** of legs and motion, leaving a tight web cable behind.

Tektonicus Max couldn't stop in time. It kept moving and the cable strained against its leg. Slowly, like a felled tree, the robot began to fall.

"You did it!" Axel cheered. "He's coming down!"

And then the cable snapped.

Tektonicus Max turned to look down at DARKWEAVER, huddled at its feet.

"Well, well, well," said Mr. Grabbem. "**I see you.** Trying to trip me, eh? Looks like this is a bug that needs to be stomped."

CHAPTER 10

Tektonicus Max raised its foot, ready to crush REAVER – and Yumi – to a pulp.

Axel had to do something, fast. "BEAST, lock missiles on that robot's eye and fire!"

The flurry of **micro missiles** struck home with sharp, popping explosions like firecrackers. Momentarily blinded, Tektonicus Max teetered on one leg. REAVER quickly skittered out from under it, sprang into the air and shifted back into his regular form before landing. *Cool move,* Axel thought.

"Where'd you go?" roared Mr. Grabbem. "That trick won't work twice!"

REAVER skidded to a halt next to BEAST. "So much for that plan," gasped Yumi.

"We've got to keep fighting. Together we can beat him, I know we can!"

"We have to combine our strength. BEAST, are you willing to use Interface X?"

Axel tried to ask, "What's Interface X?" but BEAST was already saying "YES!"

"REAVER?" Yumi asked.

"I ... AM WILLING."

"Okay, Axel. Get ready. We're going into two-player mode!"

Axel couldn't contain himself. "Yumi, what are you talking about?"

"Show him, BEAST."

An icon Axel had never seen before lit up. It showed two half circles clicking together to form a whole.

Axel took a deep breath and pressed it.

Both BEAST and REAVER went as stiff as boards. BEAST reached out his left hand. REAVER took it with his right. Their fingers interlocked. The machinery inside their bodies hummed in harmony.

Tektonicus Max loomed over the buildings. The blackened eyeball swiveled to look right at them.

"INTERFACE X ACTIVATED," said BEAST and REAVER together.

What happened next happened **amazingly fast.** In a juddering rush that threw Axel around inside his cockpit like an astronaut in a crashing spaceship, BEAST and REAVER *fused.* At first BEAST looked like he was riding on REAVER's back, but then BEAST's legs merged with REAVER's arms. Their bodies flowed together like a complicated animation. Axel's cockpit module nestled next to Yumi's and locked in place, so they were suddenly sitting side by side. She flashed him a **quick grin,** as if she did this kind of thing all the time.

Where there had been two robots, there was one double-sized one. It had BEAST's eyes and REAVER's snarling mouth and lashing tail from his dinosaur form. It held the GALAHAD sword in a two-handed grip.

"I didn't know he could do this!" Axel said, amazed.

"Nor do Grabbem," said Yumi. "My mother baked some secrets into the shifter technology. It's just a matter of knowing how to unlock them."

◂▮▮▮▸

Like a cheat code, thought Axel. *Too cool for words.*

Mr. Grabbem was confused. He didn't understand why the two robots had merged into one big one, but as if that weren't enough his own robot was **glowing,** and he didn't think it was supposed to do that.

"The reactor's going critical," said Yumi. "I think we've only got **one shot** at this."

"Let's take it."

They each gripped their controls. Axel didn't need to ask Yumi if she was a gamer, and she didn't need to ask him. It was obvious. This was a co-op situation now. They both knew exactly what to do. Under their joint control, the BEAST/REAVER fusion ran down the street toward the oncoming giant.

Tektonicus Max drew back its fist to strike. Golden twinkles of lethal energy fell from it like toxic fairy dust. The Phoenix Reactor in its chest **throbbed** and seemed to moan with hunger.

The fused robot leapt up into the air, propelled by the twin power of REAVER's leg pistons and BEAST's foot thrusters. As Tektonicus Max's fist **swung slowly** through the air, the robot leapt gracefully onto it, using it as a stepping stone.

Mr. Grabbem stared in horror. How could anything *move* like that?

Then the fused robot was moving again. It launched itself from its first perch, spun through the air to gather momentum and **swung** the crystal sword at Tektonicus Max's neck.

Mr. Grabbem squealed and threw his hands up over his face as he saw the fused robot coming for him.

The sword bit deep. Tektonicus Max stopped in its tracks ... but its head didn't. It kept going, rolling off the neck and plunging to the ground with a **crash.** Axel and Yumi heard Mr. Grabbem's despairing cry as he fell.

Axel quickly thrust the fused robot's hand down inside Tektonicus Max's gaping neck, grabbed the Phoenix Reactor and pulled it out. The **blinding golden light** steadily dimmed to a more peaceful glow.

The two robots separated and were left standing on the headless robot's shoulders. Axel realized he was still holding the reactor. He held it out to Yumi.

"This belongs to you."

She took it. "Thanks for helping me get it back."

"You're welcome."

Yumi frowned. "Be honest, Axel. Helping me wasn't your original mission, was it?"

"No. I was meant to take the reactor for myself, to help the fight against Grabbem."

"I thought so," Yumi sighed. "You going to try fighting me again?"

"Nah. It's yours, not mine. Can't just help yourself to something because it's cool, you know?"

"Good call. Well, see you around, I guess."

"Wait. REAVER got damaged when we were fighting. I'd like to fix that."

"Oh?"

"Shift REAVER into a form that can fly and follow me," Axel said. "We're going to the **Meatball.** I want to introduce you to a friend of mine."

"Meatball?" Yumi laughed in disbelief. "Now this I have to see ..."

It was many hours before Axel headed for home. Yumi had left earlier in a repaired REAVER, taking the Phoenix Reactor with her, bound for a new top-secret location. Agent Omega had made a solemn promise to work together with the Minamoto family in the future, and to share information about the Grabbem threat.

"I think we've made an ally," Omega said, after Yumi was gone. "Possibly even a friend. **Good work down there.**"

Now Axel was flying BEAST toward his house. It was dark, but they didn't have BLACKBAT loaded, so they weren't exactly **stealthy.** (Slicing their way in with Galahad wouldn't be an option because Nedra'd seen quite enough damage done to the house already!)

Then Axel almost had a panic attack. There were relatives *everywhere*. The twins were out front, playing with his old skateboard. Kyle was in the backyard yet again. Aunt Vicki and his mom were on the deck. There was no way to reach the secret lair without being seen.

Or maybe there was.

"BEAST, I need you to shift into BLINKER."

"AGENT OMEGA SAID BLINKER WAS ONLY FOR EMERGENCIES."

Axel thought of what Aunt Vicki would say if she saw BEAST coming. "This is *definitely* an emergency."

BEAST shifted into BLINKER, a small squat form with huge ears and something round like a satellite dish sticking out of its back.

As they began to drop out of the sky, Axel lined up their first – and possibly last – teleport jump. With any luck, they should appear right in the secret lair ...

ZZZWHUMP.

Axel looked around at the familiar objects – computer, ping-pong table, couch – and sighed in relief. "We made it."

Then he saw Amali sitting on the couch, looking at him.

Axel's head went into a **spin.** He popped open BEAST's canopy and climbed out. He coughed. "Um, this is, ah, how to explain? Maybe I should start at the beginning ..."

"Hi, Axel," said Amali. "Don't worry, everything's cool. I've prepped you a cover story. My mom thinks we've been down here for hours doing computer stuff."

Axel gawped. "Seriously?"

"No problem. I like your robot, by the way. Hello again, robot."

"HELLO," said BEAST.

"Wait. You *knew* about all this?" Axel said.

"Came down here on day one, looking for a place to practice singing," Amali said. "The acoustics are pretty sick ... what, you think I'd rat you out or something?"

Axel laughed and shook his head. "I remember when you used to play with little ponies, Amali. When did you get **cool?**"

She gave him a dark look. "Hey. Don't disrespect the ponies, or there will be trouble."

Later that night, long after all the cousins were in bed and BEAST had shut down to recharge, Axel was making a Skype call. As he clicked on **Yumi Minamoto's** name, he thought back to how the day had begun, and how **alone** he'd felt in the world. A lot of things could change in only a day.

Yumi accepted the call. When Axel saw her serious face appear, he felt a lump of cold fear in his chest.

"Is everything okay? Did the reactor …?"

"The reactor's safe. Don't worry about that. Axel, **we need to talk.**"

"Talk? About what?"

"I told my mother all about you, and she was shocked when I said your last name. **Brayburn.** She'd heard that name before."

A tingle was spreading up Axel's body, as if he were being lowered slowly into **icy** water.

His mouth had gone dry. He couldn't speak. He already knew what Yumi was going to say next.

"Axel ... we think we know what happened to your dad."

THE END
(for now)

ABOUT THE AUTHOR & ILLUSTRATOR

ADRIAN C. BOTT is a gamer, writer and professional adventure-creator. He lives in Sussex, England, with his family and is allowed to play video games whenever he wants.

ANDY ISAAC lives in Melbourne, Australia. He discovered his love of illustration through comic books when he was eight years old, and has been creating his own characters ever since.